Trouble

Chris Kreie

illustrated by Tuesday Mourning

Librarian Reviewer
Marci Peschke, Librarian

Reading Consultant
Mary Evenson, Teacher

Raintree

www.raintreepublishers.co.uk
Visit our website to find out
more information about
Raintree books.

To order:
☎ Phone 0845 6044371
🖷 Fax +44 (0) 1865 312263
🖥 Email myorders@capstonepub.co.uk

Customers from outside the UK please telephone +44 1865 312262

Raintree is an imprint of Capstone Global Library Limited, a company
incorporated in England and Wales having its registered office at 7 Pilgrim
Street, London, EC4V 6LB – Registered company number: 6695582

"Raintree" is a registered trademark of Pearson Education Limited,
under licence to Capstone Global Library Limited

Text © Stone Arch Books, 2009
First published in United Kingdom by Capstone Global Library in 2010
The moral rights of the proprietor have been asserted.

Edited in the UK by Laura Knowles
Art Director: Heather Kindseth
Cover Graphic Designer: Heather Kindseth
Interior Graphic Designer: Kay Fraser
Originated by Capstone Global Library
Printed and bound in China by Leo Paper Products Ltd

ISBN 978 1 406 21389 8 (hardback)
14 13 12 11 10
10 9 8 7 6 5 4 3 2 1

ISBN 978 1 406 21410 9 (paperback)
14 13 12 11 10
10 9 8 7 6 5 4 3 2 1

British Library Cataloguing in Publication Data
Kreie, Chris -- Tennis trouble
A full catalogue record for this book is available from the British
Library.

CONTENTS

✳ CHAPTER 1

TADPOLE

Alexis Fletcher rolled the tennis ball around in her fingers. She bounced it three times on the court. Then she tossed the ball into the sky.

Whoosh!

Her arm came forwards. Her wrist snapped like a whip.

Alexis hit the ball hard. It bounced inside the four straight lines of the service box, just across the net.

The ball quickly sailed past the arm of her opponent. Then it crashed loudly into the fence behind the court.

"Wow! Do that again," shouted the coach, Miss Taylor, walking next to the court.

Alexis tossed another ball up. *Whoosh!* Again, the ball landed in the service box before bouncing sharply to the left. The other player didn't have a chance.

As Miss Taylor watched, Alexis hit over several more serves. It seemed that her plan to impress the coach was working.

Miss Taylor was the coach of the school tennis team. Today was the trials to find out who would be on the team.

Alexis was only in Year 8. She'd thought long and hard about even coming to the trials.

She had worried that trying to get into the under-18s team when she was only 13 was a mistake. What if the older girls made her look bad?

After several more great serves, Alexis looked around. Many of the other players were crowded around, watching her.

"Hey, Miss Taylor. Mind if I step in?" Olivia Hamilton asked, walking over towards the court. Alexis knew that Olivia was the best player on the team.

"Sure, Olivia," said Miss Taylor. "Go ahead."

The tall sixth-form girl trotted on to the court. "Let me see what you've got!" Olivia shouted at Alexis.

Alexis took a deep breath. Olivia seemed really tough.

Alexis served the ball towards Olivia, who pulled her racket back, preparing for a forehand shot.

Olivia made one quick step to her right. She smashed the ball back across the net.

Alexis jerked to her left, but it was too late. She missed.

"Hey, Tadpole," shouted Morgan Anderson, another sixth-former. "No more tricks up your sleeve now that you've got some real competition, huh?"

Alexis tried to ignore her new nickname. She took a deep breath and got ready for another serve.

"Same as before, Olivia!" Morgan shouted.

Smash! Alexis served the ball high above her head.

Olivia took a giant step to her right, but the ball whizzed by her racket and into the fence. The other players hooted and shouted.

"Okay, players," shouted Miss Taylor. "Bring it in."

Alexis heard Morgan say, "You'll get her next time, Olivia." She patted Olivia on the back and narrowed her eyes at Alexis.

"Well done today, all of you," said Miss Taylor. "I think this year is going to be great."

"You should all be proud of yourselves," she said. "I hate to leave anyone out, but I have to. So, check the notice board tomorrow morning for the list of players who made it on to the team. If you didn't make it this year, I hope to see you back next year."

The girls jogged off the court. Another player ran up alongside Alexis. "Hi. You're Alexis, right? I'm Ellie. You were amazing out there today."

"Thanks," said Alexis.

"No, really, you were great," Ellie said. "Everyone said they'd never seen anything like it."

Alexis was shocked, and proud. "Really?" she asked shyly.

Ellie nodded. "You're going to make the under-18s team for sure, and you're only in Year 8!" she said. "That's brilliant. I'll be happy just to make the Year 10 team. But under-18s? Wow."

"We'll see," said Alexis, smiling.

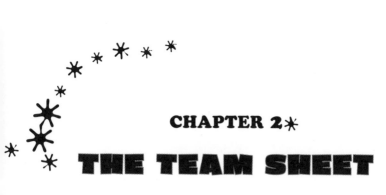

CHAPTER 2 ✳

THE TEAM SHEET

The next day Alexis got to school early. She couldn't wait to check the team sheet. As she walked towards the changing room, she saw a group of girls gathered outside.

Ellie stepped out of the crowd and ran up to Alexis. "Congratulations! I told you you'd make the under-18s team!" she said.

Alexis hardly believed her. "Are you sure?" she asked.

Ellie nodded, smiling. Alexis let out a deep breath. Her dream to play tennis for the school was coming true!

"What about you?" she asked Ellie.

Ellie smiled widely. "I got on the doubles team!" she said.

Just then, Olivia and Morgan walked up. "Step aside, girls," said Morgan. She waited for a few seconds for the crowd to part. Then she and Olivia walked up to the notice board.

Olivia and Morgan looked at the team list. When they turned around, neither of them looked happy.

"Tadpole!" said Morgan, looking out at the crowd. "You've got to be kidding me! Tadpole made it on to the under-18s team? Has Miss Taylor lost her mind?"

Then she walked over to Alexis and said, "So, I bet you think you're pretty amazing, making the under-18s team when you're what, 10?"

"I'm 13," said Alexis.

"Well, good for you," said Morgan. "You know what you did yesterday? You knocked one of my friends off the team."

"I'm really sorry," Alexis said quietly. "I didn't mean to." She saw Olivia comforting a girl who had tears in her eyes.

Morgan shook her head. "Oh, you didn't mean to?" she said angrily. "Well, it doesn't matter. Thanks to you, Rachel got knocked off the team. This is her final year. This was her last chance. And because of you, she'll never get to play under-18s."

Alexis felt awful. She didn't know what to do or say next.

"Are you just going to stand there?" asked Morgan. She stepped even closer to Alexis. Alexis saw Morgan clench her fists.

Olivia raced over. "Come on, Mo," she said. "It's not worth it." She pulled Morgan away. "Let's go."

Ellie looked at Alexis and said, "Wow, nice way to start the year."

Olivia looked Alexis in the eyes. Then she shook her head and followed Morgan through the changing room door.

* CHAPTER 3

NUMBER FOUR

Before practice that afternoon, Alexis and Ellie warmed up together.

"You're really good, Ellie!" shouted Alexis across the net. She hit a backhand shot, reaching across her body to the left to hit the ball.

"Thanks," said Ellie. "I'm better at doubles, though. Then I get to spend a lot of time hitting volleys up at the net. Go ahead. Hit me some."

Ellie went closer to the net. She returned Alexis's shots, smacking each one back with a crisp, sharp volley.

Alexis was impressed. "Nice," she said.

"So, are you still worried about Morgan?" Ellie asked, continuing to return Alexis's shots.

"Kind of," Alexis replied. "She seemed really mad earlier."

"Forget about her," Ellie said. "Her bark's worse than her bite."

"But is it true?" Alexis asked slowly. "Did I knock Rachel off the team?"

"Well, sort of," Ellie admitted. "But it's not your fault. Miss Taylor wants the best players to play on the team, and you're one of the best."

Alexis hit a ball hard along the sideline. Ellie couldn't even touch it with her racket.

"Nice shot," yelled Ellie.

"What about Olivia?" asked Alexis. "She seems okay."

"She's nice. I don't know why she's friends with Morgan, though," Ellie said. She shook her head.

"She didn't seem too happy with me being on the team either," said Alexis.

"Olivia, Morgan, and Rachel planned on being on the team together this year. Now they aren't," Ellie said, shrugging.

"Okay, girls. Bring it in!" yelled Miss Taylor. The players gathered around the coach. She said, "Welcome to the first practice of the under-18s tennis team!"

The girls all clapped. Miss Taylor said, "Congratulations to all of you for making the team. I'm not going to waste any time. I'm going to give you your positions right away, and then let you challenge each other to move up to higher spots during the season."

Alexis knew what that meant. Each girl would be ranked in order of talent. If someone wanted to get a better rank, she'd have to play for it.

After calling out the doubles teams, Miss Taylor read off the singles positions. "At number four will be Alexis, number three will be Stephanie, number two is Morgan, and number one is Olivia," she finished, smiling. "Congratulations, Olivia. You've earned it. Now make us proud this year."

"Thanks, Miss," said Olivia. "I will."

"Now, about the challenges," said Miss Taylor. "You can make two per week. And you can only challenge the player directly above you in the ranks. You play a one-set match. If the girl with the lower position wins, she moves to the higher position. Simple. Got it?"

All of the players nodded.

"All right then, let's get training," Miss Taylor said. "Twenty laps around the courts!"

Alexis couldn't stop smiling. Number four in her first year on the under-18s team, and as a 13-year-old? It was a dream come true.

✳ CHAPTER 4

FIRST MATCH

Two weeks after the first practice, Alexis looked across the net at her opponent. She was playing against a girl from Oakley Community School in the first match of the year.

The first player to win two sets would win the match. Alexis had lost the first set of the match. But in the second set, Alexis had come back to beat her opponent six games to four. Then the match was tied.

So far in the third set, Alexis had won four games to her opponent's five. She was close to losing the match. Her opponent only needed to win one more game to win the match.

Alexis wished she was serving, but it was the other player's turn to serve. The player who served always had more control over the outcome of the game. Alexis didn't like to give up that control, especially when she needed to win this game.

Alexis was ahead. But her opponent came back with two sharp serves. The game was tied.

Alexis was ready to receive the next serve. She bounced on the balls of her feet and waited. The ball flew across the net and curved directly at her.

In a flash, Alexis took two giant steps backwards and hit a shot across the net. It landed at her opponent's feet. The girl couldn't hit the ball back.

The score was 30–40. Alexis was one point away from winning the game and tying the set at five games to five.

Alexis got into position to receive the next serve. The ball was up high. Alexis tried to end the game with one shot. But she hit the ball too hard, too flat, and into the net.

Alexis planned to keep the ball in play on the next two points. If she could hit good shots, she could wait for her opponent to make a mistake.

She never had the chance. First, Alexis accidentally hit the ball into the net.

On the next point, her opponent hit a serve so hard that Alexis didn't even touch it with her racket. It was an ace.

Just like that, the match was over.

Alexis jogged up to the net. She shook hands with her opponent. Then she left the court.

"Well done," said Ellie, who was waiting on the sidelines. "You almost did it."

"Yeah," said Alexis. "But I didn't even win a game in the first set. I was so nervous."

"That's okay," Ellie said. "These girls are tough. Only one girl on our team has won so far."

"Who's still playing?" Alexis asked.

"Olivia," said Ellie. "Let's go and watch."

Olivia was in the middle of a tough match. She was playing against the other team's number one singles player.

"That girl was on the doubles team that won the championship last year," said Ellie as she and Alexis neared the court. "She must have switched over to singles this year."

"Let's go, Olivia!" yelled Morgan from the sidelines. "Show her what you've got!"

"Morgan lost too," said Ellie.

Olivia was amazing to watch. She moved quickly on the court, hitting back nearly everything her opponent could send to her.

"Whoa, Olivia is good," said Alexis.

"Tell me about it," said Ellie. "But you're as good as she is."

"No way," Alexis said.

"You are. I can't wait to see the two of you play," Ellie replied. "When you challenge her for the number one spot."

Alexis glared at Ellie. "Come off it," she said. "I don't plan on challenging Olivia."

Olivia served the ball. When it came sailing back, Olivia smacked it deep into the court. She moved to the net.

Her opponent went for a lob, trying to hit the ball over Olivia's head. The ball sailed towards Olivia.

Olivia leapt up. She extended her arm for a backhand smash.

It was an extremely tricky shot. To do it right, Olivia had to turn her back to the net, jump as high as she could, and hit the ball above her head and backwards.

She did it easily. The ball slammed into the far court and away from her opponent. Olivia had won.

Ellie looked at Alexis. "You and Olivia. It's going to be a good match," she said.

✳ CHAPTER 5

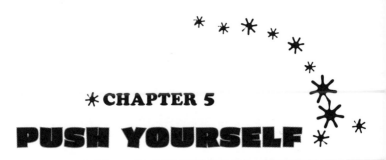

PUSH YOURSELF

A few weeks later, Rachel challenged
Alexis to a friendly match for the third
time. And for the third time, Alexis
beat her.

After the match, Alexis went to the end
court to grab some water.

"Beat her again?" asked Ellie from
behind the fence.

"Yeah," Alexis said.

"Well, don't act so excited!" Ellie said, smiling.

"I kind of feel bad for her," Alexis admitted. "You know, since she's a sixth-former and everything. I'd probably hate me too if I was in her shoes."

"She doesn't hate you," said Ellie. "Besides, you're better than she is. That's clear. What are you going to do, let her win?"

Just then, Miss Taylor yelled, "Alexis! Come over here!"

"Uh-oh," said Ellie, laughing. "You're in trouble."

Alexis jogged over to the benches and sat down next to her coach.

"How are things going?" asked Miss Taylor. "Are you enjoying yourself?"

"Yeah," said Alexis. "I love playing tennis. And it's really cool to be on the under-18s team."

"Good," Miss Taylor said. "You're a very talented player."

"Thanks," Alexis said.

"So, Alexis. When do you plan to challenge Stephanie for the number three spot?" Miss Taylor asked.

"I'm not sure," Alexis replied. "I don't mind being number four. I think that's a good spot for me."

"Alexis, you and I both know you're better than that," Miss Taylor said. Her voice was serious. She went on, "I put you at number four was because I wanted to see you earn a higher ranking. But now I'm a little disappointed."

"Oh," Alexis said. She felt awful. "I'm sorry, Miss."

Miss Taylor relaxed a little. "Don't be sorry. Just push yourself. I want to see you push yourself, and you aren't."

"But I'm only 13!" Alexis said. "I'm happy just being on the team."

"That's not good enough for me, Alexis," Miss Taylor told her. "I want to see you be your best."

"But, Miss, the older players can't stand me already. If I start challenging them, they'll really hate me," Alexis said.

Miss Taylor shook her head. "That's their problem, not yours," she said. "Did you know that Morgan beat two 17-year-olds when she was only 15 to earn the number three spot?"

"No," Alexis admitted. "I had no idea."

"She's been there. So have the other girls," Miss Taylor said. She smiled at Alexis. "Just tell me you'll think about it."

"Okay," Alexis said finally. "I'll challenge Stephanie."

✳ CHAPTER 6

INTIMIDATION

At practice the next week, Alexis and Ellie hit ground strokes back and forth across the net.

"Nice match with Stephanie the other day," said Ellie. "You thrashed her. I'm so glad you decided to start making some challenges for a higher rank. Now everyone will really be able to see what you can do."

Alexis ran down a ball in the corner and hit it back to Ellie.

"It's not a big deal," said Alexis. "I really just want to play tennis."

"Are you sure about that?" Ellie asked, smiling. "You're challenging Morgan today for the number two spot, aren't you? Something tells me you want to do a little more than just play tennis."

"Be quiet and hit the ball, will you?" Alexis said with a laugh.

Ellie hit a shot that pushed Alexis behind the baseline, which marked the end of the court. Alexis stepped back and hit the ball.

Ellie hit another shot, and another. Each time, she pushed Alexis further and further behind the baseline.

"You don't have to hit it that well!" said Alexis, out of breath.

Then Ellie stepped into the ball and hit it hard. She moved her racket quickly under the ball. The ball barely cleared the net. Finally, it landed several steps in front of Alexis.

Alexis didn't have a chance. She almost fell over as she tried to get to the net. The ball bounced a couple of times before it finally stopped.

A voice came from the next court. "You need to move up on those, you know." Alexis looked up. It was Olivia.

"Those big shots deep in the court that drive you behind the baseline," Olivia went on. "You need to move up on those. Don't get so far behind the baseline. That's the problem you're having."

"Yeah?" Alexis replied nervously.

"Let me show you," Olivia said. She ran over to Ellie's side of the net. "May I?" she asked.

"Sure," said Ellie, stepping out of the way.

"Go ahead," Olivia told Alexis. "Hit me some deep shots."

Alexis hit a huge shot. It flew deep into Olivia's court.

Then Olivia stepped up. She barely waited for the ball to drop. Then she immediately smacked it back across the net and past Alexis's racket.

"You can't wait for the ball to bounce so high," said Olivia. "You need to get the ball right after it bounces. Otherwise, your opponent will drive you too far behind the baseline."

"Okay," Alexis said. "Thanks."

"So, you're taking on Morgan today?" Olivia asked.

"Yeah," Alexis replied.

Olivia smiled and said, "Just remember, Morgan's going to try to intimidate you. Don't let her."

"Why are you telling me this?" Alexis asked, feeling confused. "You want me to win?"

"No," Olivia said. "I just don't want to see you lose to someone intimidating you. You shouldn't lose that way."

"Hey, Tadpole!" yelled Morgan from the next court. "Let's play."

"Besides," Olivia added, "even if you beat Morgan, you're never going to get past me for the top spot." She winked at Alexis.

Alexis smiled. "Right," she said. "Well, I have to go and beat Morgan now."

Then Alexis jogged to the next court, where Morgan was waiting.

CHAPTER 7 *

CHALLENGING MORGAN

After playing for nearly an hour, Alexis was ahead of Morgan five games to four. Just one more game, and she would win the set.

Because this was a challenge match, not an actual match, they didn't play best two out of three sets like they did in matches with other schools. Alexis only needed to win this one set to win the match. That would make it easier for her to win the challenge.

Alexis felt very confident, mainly because it was her turn to serve. Morgan had struggled against her serve all match.

Alexis opened with a hard serve. Morgan hit a forehand back. "Try to get that one, Tadpole!" she yelled.

Alexis hit a shot deep into Morgan's court. Then she moved to the net.

Morgan stepped forwards. She got ready to hit the ball.

"Here it comes," Morgan yelled. She smacked the ball and delivered a winner into the far corner.

The score was Love–15. Morgan had won the first point.

Alexis tried not to get too nervous. It was only one point. Nothing to worry about. She could still win.

Following her next serve, Alexis quickly ran to the net. She wanted to shorten the distance. Hopefully, that would help her get to Morgan's next shot before it even had a chance to bounce. Just the way Olivia had told her.

Morgan drilled the ball right at Alexis. The shot was easy. Alexis pounced on it and hit it for a winner. The score was tied at 15–15.

Alexis looked around. Most of the players on the other courts had stopped playing. They were all watching her play against Morgan.

Morgan won the next point by getting to the net really quickly and slamming a shot that went far out of Alexis's reach. The score was 15–30.

On the next point, Alexis didn't waste any time. She hit a serve hard, right at Morgan's body.

Morgan barely got out of the way of the ball, but couldn't manage to hit it over the net. The score was tied, 30–30.

"Two more points," thought Alexis. "Just put two more good points together and the match will be over."

Alexis lined up her serve and took a deep breath. She hit the ball high above her head. Morgan waited and sent the ball back towards Alexis.

Alexis tried to stay calm. "Hit good shots," she thought. "Don't go for too much. Take it easy."

She hit a soft shot back to Morgan. Then she went to the net.

Morgan tried to hit a lob over Alexis's head, but it was nowhere near high enough.

Alexis stepped back and went into a motion that looked a lot like her serve. She reached up high with her arm and slammed the ball across the net. It hit the ground several steps away from Morgan.

Alexis pumped her fist. "Yes!" she yelled happily.

Alexis looked at Ellie. She and the girls around her were going nuts. The score was 40–30.

"One more point," Alexis thought. "Just one more point." She took a deep breath and got ready to serve.

Alexis served. Morgan returned it with a forehand that she smashed deep into Alexis's court.

Alexis played it on her back foot. Morgan hit another one deep. Alexis took another step backwards and punched the ball across the net. Morgan grunted and hit another huge forehand.

Then Alexis remembered Olivia's advice: *Attack the ball. Don't let it attack you.*

Alexis lunged forwards and hit the ball. As it flew to Morgan's side of the court, Alexis ran up towards the net.

Morgan reached out and hit the ball back with a weak backhand.

Alexis was waiting. She took a step forwards and sent the ball away from Morgan. The match was over.

Ellie ran on to the court. Alexis smiled as her friend hugged her. "Great job!" Ellie said. "That was a brilliant game."

Morgan slammed her tennis racket into the ground. The racket bounced up and smacked Morgan in the elbow.

Olivia walked on to the court and put her arm around Morgan. "Don't worry, Mo," she said. "You'll get her next time."

Olivia walked with Morgan off the court. But as she did, she turned around and gave Alexis a tiny smile.

CHAPTER 8 ✳

THE BIG TIME

Two weeks later, the team minibus pulled into the car park of Churchill School.

"So, how many years has it been since we've won a match against this lot?" asked Alexis.

"Eleven," Ellie said. "In other words, practically our whole lives."

The minibus squeaked to a stop. One by one, the girls got out.

Alexis looked around at the freshly mown grass and the neatly trimmed trees. The tennis courts were surrounded by flowers. The school was really nice. Alexis let out a deep breath. This was the big time.

"Well, if it isn't Motormouth Morgan," said one of the Churchill team's players.

"Good to see you, too, Huffer," said Morgan. "Ready to lose and cry like a baby?"

"Oh, you mean like you did last year?" the player replied. Her teammates around her laughed.

Ellie whispered to Alexis, "That's Lidya Huffington. Last year Morgan had six match points against her and still lost. It was pretty bad."

"Prepare to look silly this year," said Morgan. "We're going to wipe the floor with you."

"Poor little Morgan," said Lidya. "She talks a good game. Too bad she can't back it up. How many times have I beaten you? Oh yeah, that's right, now I remember. Five."

Morgan laughed. "Whatever," she said.

"I hear there's a 13-year-old playing against me this year," said Lidya. "Are you really that scared of me?"

"Nah, just tired of you, that's all," Morgan said.

"Nice racket, by the way," said Lidya. "I see you saved up for the expensive one from the supermarket." She turned and walked away.

Morgan stared into Alexis's eyes and said, "Tadpole, you'd better beat her. Understood?"

"Understood," said Alexis.

"Good," Morgan said. "I'll see you after the match, when we celebrate our team win."

∗ CHAPTER 9

A TRUE TEAMMATE

Alexis felt great.

Her backhand was working. Her forehand was working. She felt like she had enough energy to play ten sets.

Alexis had beaten Lidya Huffington easily in the first set, winning six games to two. And in the second set, Alexis was on track to win the match. She was ahead five games to one. She knew she would win the last game too.

It was Alexis's serve. She bounced the ball, tossed it, and then sent it across the net.

Lidya hit it back low, but Alexis was able to knock it back. She quickly moved up to the net.

Lidya hit a weak shot, which Alexis returned easily for a point. Alexis was ahead. The score was 15–Love.

"Finish it off," someone said.

Alexis turned around. It was Morgan. Olivia was standing next to her.

"How did you guys do?" asked Alexis.

"We won," said Morgan. "Of course."

"So far, all of us have won," said Olivia. "If you beat Lidya, we'll win all of the matches."

Alexis nodded. Then she turned back to face Lidya.

Alexis served to Lidya's forehand. Lidya fired a deep ball back. Alexis attacked it and sent a shot deep to Lidya's backhand. Lidya hit it back.

Alexis hit the next shot to Lidya's forehand, forcing her to run to the opposite corner. Lidya barely got her racket on the ball.

Then Alexis moved forward and swung at the ball in mid-air. She hit the ball deep into the court and away from Lidya. The score was 30–Love.

Alexis lined up her next serve. She decided to go for a big serve to Lidya's right that would take her out of position and leave most of the court open.

It worked.

Lidya hit a weak shot back to Alexis. Alexis stepped into the shot and drilled it into the open court. The score was 40–Love. Alexis was winning.

"Go, Alexis!" Ellie yelled. Alexis looked behind her. Olivia and Morgan were still watching too.

Alexis took a deep breath. She bounced the ball three times.

Then she went for it. Her racket flew through the air and struck the ball. In a flash, the ball cleared the net, landed in the service box, and bounced past Lidya's swinging racket.

Lidya's racket didn't even touch the ball. It was another one of Alexis's famous aces. It was also match point.

Alexis had won!

The players behind Alexis went nuts.

After shaking hands with Lidya, Alexis ran off the court. All of her teammates were there, cheering for her. The players all hugged her at once.

"Alexis," said Olivia, "that was awesome. You're a true teammate."

Morgan stood behind the crowd. "Are you all quite finished?" she said. The other players looked at Morgan and went quiet.

Morgan smiled and stepped towards Alexis. She held up her hand. Alexis slapped it as hard as she could.

Morgan nodded her head. "Not bad, Tadpole," she said. "Not bad at all."

✳ ABOUT THE AUTHOR ✳

Chris Kreie grew up playing tennis on his local, run-down tennis court. It wasn't until his final year that his secondary school started a tennis team. Chris joined the team and has been playing tennis ever since. Chris has a wife and two children. He works as a school librarian, and in his free time he writes books like this one.

✳ ABOUT THE ILLUSTRATOR ✳

When Tuesday Mourning was a little girl, she knew she wanted to be an artist when she grew up. Now, she is an illustrator who is especially keen on working on books for children and teenagers. When she isn't illustrating, Tuesday loves spending time with her husband, who is an actor, and their son, Atticus.

GLOSSARY

challenge   invite someone to try to beat you at something

competition   contest

confident   having a strong belief in one's own abilities

disappointed   let down because something hasn't happened as planned

expensive   costing a lot of money

intimidate   frighten

opponent   person who is against you in a contest

position   place where someone is

rank   order of ability. The better your ability, the higher your rank.

TENNIS WORDS YOU SHOULD KNOW

Tennis, like most sports, has some words with special meanings. Here are some of the words used in tennis. These words were all used in this book.

ace point won with one hit

backhand a stroke that starts on the opposite side of the body from the arm that holds the racquet

baseline line at the back of the tennis court

doubles a way of playing tennis with two people on each side of the net

forehand a stroke that starts with the palm facing the way the stroke will move

game one part of a tennis set

lob hit a ball high into the air

Love in tennis, a score of Love means zero points

match entire contest between two players

match point the point that wins the match

racket paddle used to hit balls in tennis

return hit the ball back to the other player

serve send the ball to the other player to begin the set

service box area of a tennis court from which a serve is played

set one part of a tennis match

sideline line on each side of a tennis court

volley shot that goes high up and can be hit before the ball bounces on the ground

Scoring note: In tennis, scoring doesn't go 0-1-2-3. Instead, it's Love-15-30-40! The player who scores two clear points after 40 wins.

DISCUSSION QUESTIONS

1. Why was Morgan mean to Alexis at the beginning of this book? What made her change at the end?

2. Alexis didn't want to challenge the older girls at first. Why not? What would you have done in her situation?

3. Should younger kids be allowed to try out for older kids' sports teams? Why or why not?

WRITING PROMPTS

1. Pretend that you're Alexis. Write a diary entry about the day at Churchill School, playing against Lidya Huffington.

2. Sometimes it can be interesting to think about a story from another person's point of view. Try rewriting chapter 8 from Morgan's point of view. What does she feel like during this chapter? What does she think? What does she see and hear?

3. Even though she was nervous, Alexis tried out for the under-18s tennis team. Write about a time when you did something even though you were nervous.

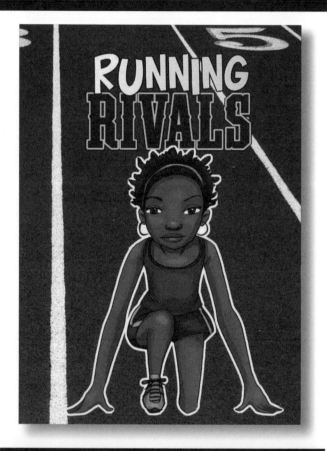

Amy hurt her knee during a race. Her knee healed, but her confidence is still broken. The biggest race of the year is coming up, and it's on the exact same track where she was hurt before. With help from an unexpected source, will she be able to race again?

Anna, Bethany, and Jasmine have a problem. There's no girls' football team at their school any more. They have to join the team at their arch rival school! The players on their new team aren't very nice. Will the girls ever feel at home?

FIND OUT MORE

Books

Maria Sharapova, Mark Stewart (Gareth
 Stevens, 2009)
Tennis, Patricia Bow (Franklin Watts, 2009)
Venus and Serena Williams, Hal
 Marcovitz (Mason Crest, 2009)

Websites

www.lta.org.uk
The Lawn Tennis Association website tells
you everything you need to know about
tennis in the UK, including finding out
about tennis in your area.

**news.bbc.co.uk/cbbcnews/hi/find_out/
guides/sport/tennis**
This six-part guide to tennis has
information on what the sport is all about,
how it started, and the major tennis
tournaments.